Polly the Party Fun Fairy

To Molly May Britton,
the party girl of Perry Barr

Special thanks to
Narinder Dhami

ISBN 978-0-545-22172-6

12 11 10 9 8 7 6 5 4 3 2 1   10 11 12 13 14 15/0

Printed in the U.S.A.   40

First Scholastic Printing, July 2010

Polly
the Party
Fun Fairy

by Daisy Meadows

SCHOLASTIC INC.

New York   Toronto   London   Auckland
Sydney   Mexico City   New Delhi   Hong Kong

The Fairyland Palace

Clearing

The Village Hall

Twisty Lane

Wetherbury Village

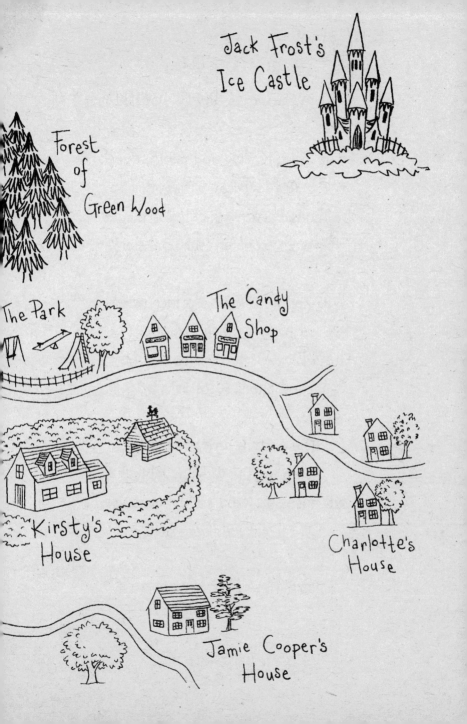

A Very Special Party Invitation

Our gracious king and gentle queen
Are loved by fairies all.
One thousand years they have ruled well,
Through troubles great and small.

In honor of their glorious reign
A party has been planned.
We'll celebrate their anniversary
Throughout all of Fairyland.

The party is a royal surprise,
We hope they'll be delighted.
So pull out your wand and fanciest dress . . .
For *you* have been invited!

RSVP: THE FAIRY GODMOTHER

Contents

Woodland Fun

"Good-bye, Mom!" Kirsty Tate called, waving from the school bus packed with Explorers as it pulled away from the school.

"Good-bye, Mrs. Tate!" Rachel Walker, Kirsty's best friend, shouted. She was waving, too.

As the school bus made its way through the village, Rachel turned to Kirsty.

"Isn't it great that your Explorers
leader is letting me come to your mini-
jamboree?" she said happily.

"Well, you *are* staying with me this week,
so there's no way I'd leave you behind!"
Kirsty laughed. "And you're an Explorer,
too, even if you're not in our troop."

Rachel nodded. Both she and Kirsty
were wearing their Explorer uniforms.
"I'm really looking forward to this," she
said eagerly. "What did you do last year?"

"We met up with another troop of Explorers—just like we're doing this time—so there were lots of us," Kirsty explained. "We played games, ran races, and there were prizes, too. Then we roasted marshmallows around the campfire." She grinned. "It really was just a big party in the woods!"

Rachel's eyes opened wide. "A party?" she gasped. "You know what that means. . . ."

Kirsty clapped a hand to her mouth. "Oh, I didn't realize!" she said. "We'll have to be on the lookout for goblins!"

Even though Kirsty and Rachel
seemed just like all the other Explorers
on the bus, the two girls had a special
secret. They had become friends with the
fairies! Now, whenever their fairy friends
were in trouble, Kirsty and Rachel tried
to help.

Trouble usually came in the shape of
cold, prickly Jack Frost and his goblins.
Now Jack Frost was doing his best to
ruin the secret party for the fairy king
and queen's 1000th anniversary. The
seven Party Fairies were helping with
the preparations. Jack Frost was trying to
stop them by sending his goblins into the
human world to ruin as many parties as
they could! Then, when the Party Fairies
came flying to the rescue, the goblins
would try to steal their magic party bags

for Jack Frost. He planned to use the Party Fairies' special magic to have a fabulous party of his own.

"Yes, we'll have to keep our eyes open," agreed Rachel, as the school bus came to a stop in a large clearing in the woods. There were already lots of Explorers milling around. The other troop had arrived! "We can't let the goblins steal any of the Party Fairies' magic bags," she added firmly.

"And we won't let them

ruin our day, either," Kirsty declared,
looking determined.

Mrs. Talbot, Kirsty's Explorers
leader, opened the door
of the bus. "Here we are,
girls," she said with a
smile. "Put your bags
under that big tree,
and then we'll start with
some races."

The Explorers on the bus cheered as
they jumped to their feet. Rachel and
Kirsty were the last to leave. As they
stepped off the bus, they both looked
carefully around the clearing for any
signs of goblin trouble, but they couldn't
see anything out of the ordinary.

"There are lots of places for goblins to
hide here," Kirsty whispered to Rachel,

as they put their bags under the giant
oak tree.

"Gather around, girls," called Mrs.
Talbot, who had been chatting with
the other Explorers leader, Mrs. Carter.
"We're going to start with an obstacle
course. We need four volunteers from
each troop."

Kirsty nudged Rachel. "That sounds like fun," she said. "Should we volunteer?"

Rachel nodded, and they both put their hands up.

"Jenny and Emily," said Mrs. Talbot, pointing at two girls. "Oh, and Kirsty and your friend, Rachel—you can be our team!"

Kirsty, Rachel, and the other girls
watched closely as Mrs. Talbot showed
them the course. First, they had to run
along a wooden balance beam. Then
they had to scramble under a net, run
along the top of a row of overturned
buckets, and make a shot through
a basketball hoop. To finish, all four
members of the team had to jump into
a rubber boat and row across the wide
stream that flowed
along one side of
the clearing.

"It looks hard,"
Kirsty said,
nervously.

"Not as hard as
trying to outwit
goblins!" Rachel replied with a laugh.

As the two teams lined up, the other
Explorers began cheering for their
teammates. Mrs. Carter blew her
whistle, and they were off!

Jenny ran lightly along the beam first,
followed by Rachel, Kirsty, and Emily.

"If anyone falls off, they have to go
back to the beginning of the plank and
start again!" Mrs. Talbot warned. But
both teams made it across safely.

Then they began to wiggle under the
net. Rachel and
Kirsty's team pulled
ahead slightly,
as one of the
Explorers on the
other team got
her barrette caught in the mesh. By the
time she was free, Rachel and Kirsty's
team had already
run along the row
of buckets, and
was trying to
shoot baskets through
the basketball hoop.

"I'm horrible at
this," Emily said
anxiously to

Kirsty, as they watched Jenny and then Rachel make baskets with their first shots.

"Don't worry," Kirsty replied. "Just do your best."

But after Kirsty had scored, it took poor Emily six more tries to get her basket. By then, the other team had almost caught up with them.

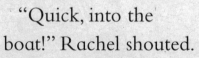

"Quick, into the boat!" Rachel shouted.

They all jumped into the little inflatable boat and grabbed the paddles. But as they pushed off from the bank, the other team was running up to their own boat.

"Paddle harder!" shouted Jenny, as they made their way to the middle of the stream.

"They're right behind us!" Kirsty gasped, glancing back.

Then, suddenly, she felt cold water seeping into her sneakers. Surprised, she looked down. Water was pouring into the boat, and she could hear the hissing sound of air escaping as the boat began to deflate. It had sprung a leak!

Egg and Spoon Surprises

"Oh, no!" Kirsty shouted. "We're sinking!"

The other girls gasped.

"We have to bail out!" cried Rachel.

"Girls!" Mrs. Talbot was standing on the bank, looking worried. "Are you all right?"

"Our boat's leaking!" Kirsty yelled, as they sank even lower in the water.

There was a shout from the Explorers in the other boat. "So is ours!"

"Quick, girls!" Mrs. Carter rolled up

her pants and waded into the stream toward them. "The water's not very deep. Take your shoes and socks off, and I'll help you climb out."

The eight girls waded to the bank,

dragging their deflated boats behind them. "Do you think this could be goblin trouble?" Kirsty whispered to Rachel. "It might be," Rachel agreed with a nod.

Mrs. Carter was examining one of the rubber boats. "Look!" she said, pointing at the bottom of a boat. "There are some thorns stuck in there. That's what made the holes. I knew I shouldn't have put the boats down next to that prickly bush."

Kirsty and Rachel looked at each other.

"Maybe it was just an accident," Rachel said with shrug.

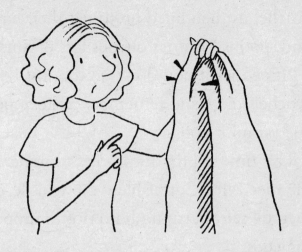

"Or maybe a goblin stuck those thorns into the boats to make them sink!" Kirsty pointed out.

"Oh, don't worry," Mrs. Talbot was saying, patting Mrs. Carter on the shoulder. "I brought a present for our pass the present game, and I don't even remember where I put it! Let's do the egg and spoon race while I look for it."

"I'm not very good at this," Kirsty told

Rachel as they lined up to get their eggs
and spoons. "But it's always lots of fun."

"It's easier if you don't go too fast,"
Rachel said, "and remember to keep your
eye on your egg."

This time, all the Explorers took part in
the race. Mrs. Carter blew the whistle, and
they all set off, trying hard not to drop
the eggs.

Rachel had a steady hand. She was soon in the lead, but Kirsty was near the back. Suddenly, Emily rushed past her, trying to catch up with the leaders. Her hand wobbled, and her egg fell and smashed on the ground. Immediately, a horrible smell filled the air.

"Ugh!" Emily shrieked, holding her nose. "My egg's rotten!"

"Yuck!" Kirsty exclaimed, covering her nose with her hand. She glanced down at her own egg to make sure it was steady, but then she noticed something very strange — her egg was beginning to crack!

Kirsty stopped in her tracks and another Explorer almost bumped into her. She stared at the egg as it cracked wide open. The two halves of the shell fell away, leaving a fluffy yellow chick sitting on Kirsty's spoon. It gave a little *cheep*! Kirsty gasped in amazement. "My egg hatched!"

Everyone forgot
the race as the
other Explorers
crowded around
to look at the
sweet, little chick.
But just then,
there was
the sound of
more eggs cracking.
Soon, five other surprised Explorers had
chicks sitting on their spoons instead of
eggs!

The two Explorer leaders could hardly
believe their eyes.

"This is very strange!" said Mrs. Carter.
"I hard-boiled the eggs for this race.
They must have gotten mixed up with
some uncooked ones."

"Do you think the goblins could have switched the eggs?" Kirsty muttered quietly to Rachel. But before Rachel could reply, Kirsty noticed that her chick had hopped off the spoon and was wandering away. "Hey, come back!" she cried.

Quite a few of the chicks had decided to make a break for freedom. The Explorers scattered to find them. Kirsty and Rachel followed Kirsty's chick into the trees.

"There he is," Kirsty said, pointing
at the roots of a tree where the chick
was pecking around in the soil. Then
she looked confused. "What's that
shimmering blue light at the bottom of
the tree?"

Rachel let out a gasp of delight.
"Kirsty, it must be Polly the Party Fun
Fairy!" she cried.

Polly Appears!

Rachel was right! As Kirsty peered at
the roots of the tree, Polly the Party Fun
Fairy fluttered up into the air, waving
her wand happily. She wore a sparkly
blue tank top and matching pants with a
purple belt. Long red hair tumbled over
her shoulders in shiny waves.

"I'm so glad to see you, girls!" she called in a silvery voice that tinkled like a bell. Her green eyes gleamed with joy. "I was hoping you'd come and find me."

"Is everything all right?" asked Kirsty, gently picking up her chick.

Polly looked sad for a moment. "Well, I lost my party bag," she said, looking around. "I'm sure I put it down here somewhere, but I can't find it." She gave a little giggle. "The other Party Fairies say I'm always losing things!"

"Maybe a goblin stole it," Rachel suggested.

"No, I don't think so." Polly shook her head, not looking worried at all. "I haven't seen a single goblin anywhere."

Kirsty and Rachel looked at each other anxiously. After what had happened at the mini-jamboree so far, they were pretty sure that there was a goblin lurking somewhere nearby. But before they had a chance to convince Polly, they heard Jenny calling from the clearing.

"Kirsty! Rachel! Where are you? We're going to play Frisbee now!"

"You go and play," Polly said with a smile. "I'll keep looking for my party bag." Rachel agreed. "But Polly, please be careful. Kirsty and I think there might be a goblin nearby."

"We'll come and see you again later," Kirsty promised. Cradling her chick in her hand, she and Rachel hurried back to join the others.

"Put your chick in here, Kirsty," said Mrs. Carter, pointing to a large cardboard box. "I'll take all of

them to the local farm later. They have a lot of free-range chickens there, so these chicks will have a good home."

Mrs. Talbot organized the Explorers into a circle, and they began throwing the Frisbee to each other. It was fun, and Kirsty and Rachel were enjoying themselves! But at the same time, they couldn't help thinking about Polly and her missing party bag. What if a goblin had gotten ahold of it?

Suddenly, one of the Explorers tossed the Frisbee very high into the air toward Kirsty. It sailed over Kirsty's head and landed in a bush under the tree where Polly was searching for her party bag.

Kirsty raced off toward the bush. "I'll get that!" she shouted. She couldn't risk Polly being spotted by any of the other girls!

"I'll help you look for it," Rachel called, running after her.

Behind them, Mrs. Talbot was saying, "Well, that's enough Frisbee for now, girls. Let's have some juice and cookies."

"Phew, that was close," Kirsty whispered, as she and Rachel stopped underneath the tree. "Where's Polly?"

"Here I am," called a tiny voice.

The girls looked up. Polly was perched on a branch above their heads, swinging her legs.

"Did you find your party bag?" asked Rachel.

Polly's shimmering wings drooped a little. "No." She sighed.

"Where could it be?" Then she brightened. "But I know where your Frisbee is," she added, pointing downward. "It's right in the middle of that bush."

"Thanks, Polly," said Kirsty. She and Rachel began to push the leaves aside,

looking around for the Frisbee. As they did, Polly suddenly cried out in alarm. The girls whirled around to face her. She pointed to a spot nearby.

"Girls, watch out! There's a goblin!"

Goblin Chase

There was a loud rustling of leaves as the goblin pushed his way out of the other side of the bush. He had Polly's bright blue party bag in one hand, and the Explorers' Frisbee in the other. Kirsty and Rachel climbed out from the bush just in time to see the goblin race off.

"Hee-hee," the goblin giggled with glee. "A party bag for Jack Frost, and a Frisbee for me. Hooray!"

"Come back, you horrible goblin!" Polly yelled. She zoomed after him, her wings fluttering so fast they were a shimmering blur. "Give me back my party bag!"

"Let's catch him, Rachel!" Kirsty cried, starting to run.

Polly, Kirsty, and Rachel followed the goblin toward the stream.

"We've got him now, girls!" Polly declared triumphantly. "Goblins hate getting their feet wet."

But the goblin wasn't giving up yet.

Panting, he flipped the Frisbee over and placed it on the water. It floated like a little boat! Then he grabbed one of the spoons the Explorers had used in the egg and spoon race and paddled across the stream, looking very proud of himself.

"Thought you'd caught me, didn't you?" he jeered, a grin stretching across his mean face. "Well, you didn't! Ha, ha, ha!" He stuck his tongue out at the girls.

"We've got to stop him," Polly said nervously. "It'll be easier if you two can fly, too." With a wave of her wand and a shower of sparkling fairy dust, Polly turned Kirsty and Rachel into fairies.

"Come on!" yelled Polly, as she flew out over the water like a beautiful blue dragonfly.

The goblin looked worried and began to row faster.

"How are we going to stop him?" Kirsty asked Rachel as they fluttered across the stream.

"I don't know," Rachel replied, looking around to see if there was anything that could help.

All of a sudden, Rachel spotted the row of upside-down buckets that had been part of the obstacle course. An idea popped into her head, and she turned and flew toward them.

Meanwhile, Polly was flying around the Frisbee-boat, as close to the goblin as she dared. She kept trying to grab her party bag back.

"Get away from me!" the goblin howled furiously, paddling even harder.

"Not until you give me my party bag back!" Polly cried in a determined voice. She swooped down toward the goblin again and reached for the bag that was laying on the floor of the boat. But, this time, the goblin swung his paddle at Polly, barely missing one of her wings.

"Oh, Polly, be careful!" Kirsty called, wondering where Rachel could be.

"Kirsty! Help me!"

Kirsty turned around to see Rachel trying to pick up one of the obstacle course buckets. Being fairy-size, Rachel was having a hard time! Kirsty fluttered over to help her friend. "What's this for?" she asked, helping Rachel lift the bucket.

"We need to get this over to the goblin," Rachel panted.

Carrying the bucket between them, the two girls flew over the stream.

The goblin had picked up the party bag now and was holding it tightly, jabbing at Polly with his spoon to keep her away.

"Turn the bucket upside down, Kirsty," Rachel whispered, as they hovered above the goblin's head. "Ready? Now let go!"

Both girls let go of the bucket at exactly the same time. It dropped right over the goblin's head, covering him to his knees!

Polly's Sparkly Secret

"Great shot, girls!" Polly laughed.
"Right on target!"

"Help!" the goblin yelled. He tried to knock the bucket off, but he couldn't because he was still holding his spoon-paddle in one hand and the party bag in the other. "It's too dark!"

Moaning and groaning to himself,
the goblin put the spoon and the party
bag down in the boat, and tried to
push the bucket off with both hands.
But Polly was ready for him. She
swooped down and waved her
wand over the goblin, showering him
with fairy dust.
Immediately, the
bucket stuck to
his head. No
matter how
much the goblin
twisted and turned,
he couldn't quite
shake it off!
"That should keep
you busy!" Polly
declared happily.

But the goblin was still determined to get away. He began to paddle again—but because he couldn't see where he was going, he ended up going around in circles. Polly and the girls laughed.

"Stop laughing!" the goblin demanded, banging the water with his spoon-paddle. Rachel flew over and took it away from him.

At the same time, Polly fluttered down and picked up her party bag from the bottom of the boat. "Thank you so much, girls,"

she said with a smile, hugging the bag
close.

"Our pleasure," Kirsty said.
"But what are we
going to do about
him?" She pointed at
the goblin, who was
still mumbling to himself
under the bucket.
"We'd better pull him and
the Frisbee to dry land,"
Rachel suggested.

Polly and the girls took hold of the
Frisbee and began towing the goblin
toward the bank.

"What are you doing?" the goblin
grumbled. "Where are you taking
me?"

"You're coming back to Fairyland with me," Polly replied, clutching her party bag tightly.

"I don't want to go to Fairyland!" The goblin pouted.

Rachel and Kirsty couldn't help giggling.

"Well, girls, you've saved the day again," Polly said, flying over to hug them both. "If the anniversary party is as much fun as I think it's going to be, it will all be thanks to you! I'd better get back to Fairyland now."

She raised her wand, but Kirsty stopped her. "Wait, Polly!" she cried. "You've got to make Rachel and me human-size again."

"Oops!" Polly laughed. "I almost forgot. You both make such good fairies!" She waved her wand, and a shower of glittering fairy dust swirled through the air and fell over both girls. A few seconds later, they were their normal size again.

"Good-bye, Polly!" Rachel smiled. "Say hi to the other Party Fairies for us."

"And to everyone in Fairyland," added Kirsty.

But to their surprise, Polly was still hovering there, looking thoughtful. "Before I go," she said, "there's just one more thing I need to do. . . ."

She opened her party bag, took out a handful of fairy dust, and tossed it into the air. As the sparkling blue dust whirled and tumbled to the ground, Rachel and Kirsty were delighted to see that it was all in the shape of tiny balloons.

"What are you doing, Polly?" Rachel asked curiously.

Polly grinned and waved her wand. As she and the goblin began to disappear in a shower of glittering fairy dust, she called, "You'll have to wait and see!" She winked at the girls. "For now, it's a secret!"

And with that, she vanished.

A Touch of Magic

Kirsty and Rachel looked at each other in surprise. At that moment, they heard Mrs. Talbot calling.

"Kirsty! Rachel! Where are you?"

Kirsty grabbed the Frisbee, and she and Rachel hurried back to join the other Explorers.

"Oh, there you are," said Mrs. Talbot.

"You were gone a long time." She looked down at the wet Frisbee. "Did it go in the stream?"

"Yes, it took us a while to get it back," Kirsty replied.

Rachel grinned. *That's true*, she thought.

"Well, eat your snack quickly," Mrs. Talbot went on. "We're going to play another game now."

"Did you find the box for pass the present?" asked Emily.

Mrs. Talbot looked a little embarrassed and shook her head. "No, I didn't. I can't figure out where it could be."

"I found it!" Mrs. Carter said, walking toward them with a large box wrapped in glittering, multicolored paper. "It was still on the bus."

Mrs. Talbot looked surprised. "That's not the box I . . ." she began doubtfully.

"Well, it must be," said Mrs. Carter. "It's the only present here."

Rachel and Kirsty glanced at each

other and smiled. Now they knew
what Polly had been up to when
she took the fairy dust out of
her party bag. This was a
magic present from Polly
the Party Fun Fairy!

"Gather around,
girls," called Mrs.
Carter. "Sit down
on the grass in a
big circle."

Kirsty and Rachel
hurried to join their
friends. Meanwhile,
Mrs. Talbot was still
looking confused. "I
don't remember using that sparkly
wrapping paper at all!" she muttered
to herself.

Mrs. Carter handed the present to the closest Explorer. "Now remember, girls, whoever's holding the present when the music stops gets to take off a layer of wrapping paper."

"I can't wait to see what's inside," Kirsty whispered to Rachel, as Mrs. Carter switched on the CD player. The Explorers passed the large package around the circle until Mrs. Talbot stopped the music. When she did, Jenny was holding the present.

All the Explorers, including Rachel and Kirsty, leaned forward eagerly as she ripped the first layer of paper off.

"Oh!" Everyone gasped. Hundreds of clear, shining bubbles floated up into the air, filling the sky overhead with rainbows. Rachel and Kirsty grinned and nudged each other. "Look at Mrs. Talbot's face," Kirsty whispered, giggling. "She can hardly believe her eyes!"

"I'm sure this can't be the present I wrapped. . . ." Mrs. Talbot was saying, but no one was paying attention to her. They were too excited to see what other wonderful surprises the present contained.

Mrs. Carter started the music again. This time, when it stopped and an Explorer removed another layer, hundreds of pieces of glittering confetti burst out of the paper. They sparkled

and floated down
onto the grass,
disappearing as
they landed.

Next, the present
stopped at an
Explorer sitting near
Kirsty. She tore off a layer
of paper, and everyone
gasped as colored sparkles shot up
into the air and burst overhead like tiny
fireworks. They filled the sky with dazzling
colors.

Just when the girls thought there
couldn't be any surprises left, the music
stopped again while Rachel was holding
the box. Taking a deep breath, she pulled
the shiny piece of paper apart.

It was the last layer. A huge pile of

candy, wrapped in colorful twists of
paper, spilled onto the grass.

The Explorers cheered.

"Thank you, Polly," Rachel whispered,
as she and Kirsty began to hand the
candy out to the other Explorers.

"We helped our fairy friends again,
and we had fun, too," Kirsty said, smiling
at Rachel. She sighed happily. "Fairy
adventures are always the best!"

Cherry, Melodie, Grace, Honey,
and Polly all have their magic
party bags back. Now Rachel
and Kirsty need to help

Phoebe

the Fashion Fairy!

Join their next adventure
in this special sneak peek. . . .

Birthday Trouble

Kirsty Tate and Rachel Walker were busy wrapping a birthday present for Kirsty's friend, Charlotte.

"There," said Kirsty, tying the ribbon. "Charlotte's going to love this silver headband. It's so pretty!"

"Are you almost ready, girls?" Mrs. Tate called up the stairs. "Dad and I have to leave in two minutes!"

"We're coming, Mom," Kirsty replied.
Then she turned to Rachel. "I can't
believe we're going to another party, can
you?" She grinned.

Rachel shook her head. "I wonder
what's going to happen this time," she
said excitedly.

Kirsty and Rachel put their party
dresses into a bag with Charlotte's
present, then rushed downstairs.

Kirsty's parents had to go out that
afternoon, so Mrs. Tate had arranged
for the girls to go to Charlotte's house
a little early.

"We've helped almost all of the Party
Fairies now," Kirsty said, as she and
Rachel walked along the road.

Rachel counted them off on her fingers.
"Cherry the Cake Fairy, Melodie the

Music Fairy, Grace the Glitter Fairy, Honey the Candy Fairy, and Polly the Party Fun Fairy," she said. "So the only two we haven't helped are . . ."

"Phoebe the Fashion Fairy and Jasmine the Present Fairy," Kirsty finished. "I wonder if we'll see one of them today."

Rachel couldn't help smiling as they walked up Charlotte's front path. "I bet we will," she said. "Those goblins won't be able to resist another chance to try to steal a magic party bag. One of them is bound to cause trouble! Then Phoebe or Jasmine will have to come and fix everything."

Kirsty rang the doorbell. A few moments later, Charlotte answered the door.

"Happy birthday!" cried Kirsty and Rachel together.

But then Kirsty noticed how sad her friend looked. "Is everything all right?" she asked, concerned.

Charlotte didn't seem to be in a birthday mood. She wasn't wearing a party dress, and she wasn't even smiling. "No," she wailed. "Everything is *not* all right. My favorite dress is ruined!"

RAINBOW magic ™

There's Magic in Every Series!

The Rainbow Fairies

The Weather Fairies

The Jewel Fairies

The Pet Fairies

The Fun Day Fairies

The Petal Fairies

The Dance Fairies

The Music Fairies

The Sports Fairies

The Party Fairies

Read them all!

■ SCHOLASTIC

www.scholastic.com

www.rainbowmagiconline.com

RMFAIRY2